This book belongs to:

_____

_____

_____

_____

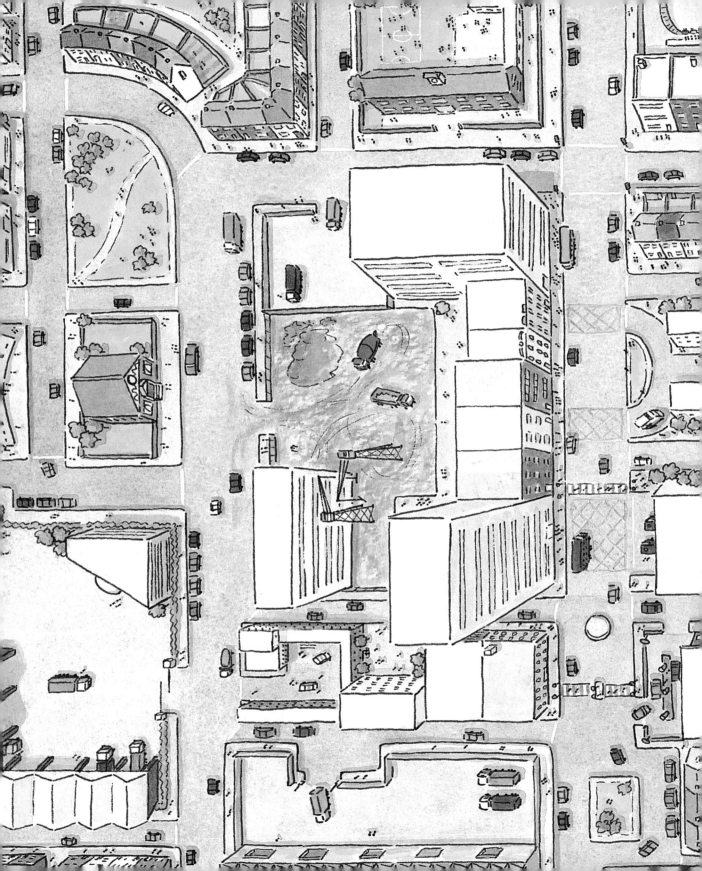

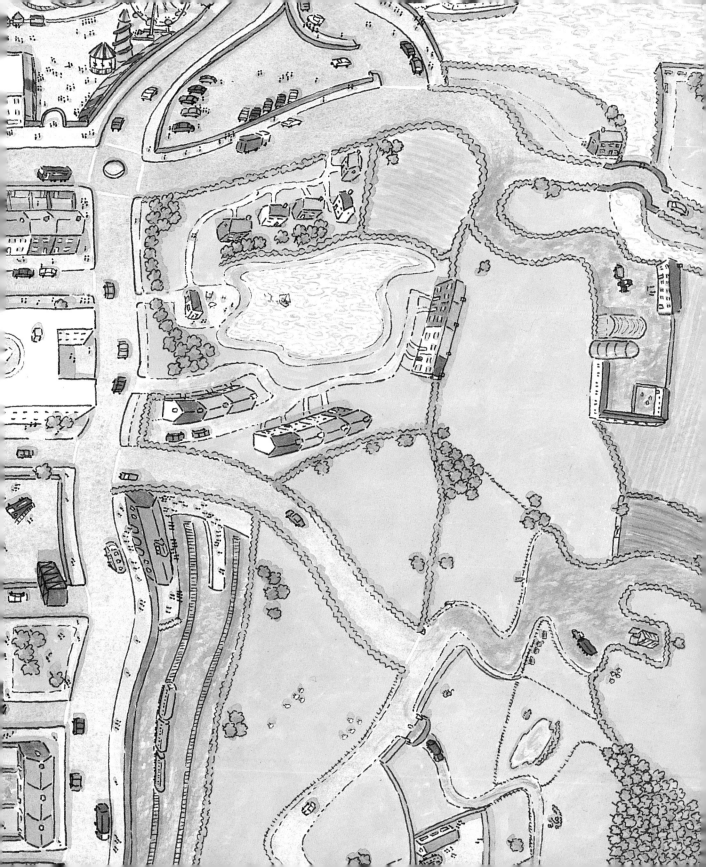

Steady Eddie and RoSPA
working together to improve road safety awareness.
To make a donation to RoSPA, please write to the
Fundraising Manager,
The Royal Society for the Prevention of Accidents
Edgbaston Park, 353 Bristol Road, Birmingham B5 7ST.

LITTLE TIGER PRESS
An imprint of Magi Publications
22 Manchester Street, London W1M 5PG
First published in Great Britain 1999
Text and illustrations © Little Tiger Press
Text by Linda Jennings
Illustrations by Sami Sweeten
Based on characters and stories by Illtyd Barrie Thomas
Steady Eddie is a registered trademark
of Stobart Management Services
Printed in Singapore by Tien Wah Press
ISBN 1 84143 002 1
1 3 5 7 9 10 8 6 4 2

STEADY EDDIE
Foils the Plot

LITTLE TIGER PRESS
London

Steady Eddie was just turning into a warehouse delivery bay when ZOOM! a battered red van shot past him, knocking over a waste-bin in its hurry. "Just look where you're going!" yelled Steady Eddie as the van sped out into the road, belching a dirty cloud of exhaust smoke behind it.

At that moment, Steady Eddie caught sight of his friend, Oliver Overdrive. He was having some big boxes loaded into him. "What are you up to?" called Steady Eddie. "You're supposed to be bringing goods into the warehouse, not taking them out."

"I'm delivering these computers to a shop in Canary
Drive," said Oliver. "The van they sent was too small
to carry them all so I said I'd take the rest."
Steady Eddie was glad that Oliver was being helpful
for once, but he hadn't liked the look of that red van,
nor the dangerous way it was being driven.

Suddenly Steady Eddie heard a lot of
noise coming from inside the warehouse.
"Of all the cheek!" cried the manager.
"Someone's just come in and stolen
a load of computers from
under our noses!"

Oh no! Steady Eddie could see it all now.
Oliver Overdrive had been fooled into handling
stolen goods. "I must warn him before the
police catch up with him," he cried. He looked
around the delivery bay, but there was no sign
of Oliver Overdrive.

"I'd better go to the police station to sort things out," groaned Steady Eddie. "Pandora the Police Car is a friend, and I'm sure she'll understand about Oliver's mistake."

"Don't worry. We'll soon catch up with Oliver Overdrive – and the real thieves," said Pandora at the police station when Steady Eddie had explained everything. "You say you have the address where Oliver was taking the computers?"

"Yes," said Steady Eddie. "It was Sparrow Close."

"Sparrow Close?" asked Pandora, puzzled.
"I've never heard of it."
"Perhaps it's Pelican Place," said Steady
Eddie. But that didn't sound right either.

"Just a minute," he said, "it's on the tip of my tongue."

"Well, we can't stand around guessing," said Pandora. "You go one way and I'll go the other. Just tell me what Oliver Overdrive looks like."

At least I know that, thought Steady Eddie thankfully.

Steady Eddie drove along, looking out for Oliver. At the same time, he was trying to remember the correct address. Woodpecker Close? Linnet Lane?

A large yellow coach was passing
by on the other side of the road.
"What a nice bright colour," thought
Steady Eddie. "Just like a canary."
He nearly honked his horn with excitement!
That was it – the name of the place –
Canary Drive!

At that moment, Steady Eddie spotted his friend, Lorretta Lorry, who drew up alongside him at the traffic lights. He interrupted her cheerful song by asking if she knew where Canary Drive was.

"It's about a mile out of town," Lorretta told him as he impatiently revved up. "Hey, Steady Eddie, you look as though you're playing cops and robbers." "I am!" called Steady Eddie as he sped away.

Steady Eddie drove on, as quickly as
he dared. Once he was out of town he saw a
rough wooden sign by the side of the road which
said 'Canary Drive'. It was no more than a dirt track.
Steady Eddie bumped along it, avoiding all the
potholes. At the very end, he saw Oliver Overdrive,
parked by an old, tumbledown barn.

"Funny-looking shop," grumbled Oliver Overdrive, as Steady Eddie drove up. "Have they given you something to deliver, too?"

"Shh," whispered Steady Eddie. "Turn off your engine, and I'll explain. But BE QUIET. I don't want that van to see us together."

"Stolen goods!" shouted Oliver, much too loudly.
"I don't believe it, I'm an honest lorry, not a thief!"

Oliver's voice had alerted the red van, which had been parked behind the barn. "Now we're for it!" groaned Steady Eddie, as the van zoomed up to them.

"Hand over those computers, or I'll bash your bonnet in!" growled the red van, screeching to a stop beside them. Oliver lost his nerve completely.

"W-what s-shall I d-do, Steady Eddie?"
he wailed.
"Don't worry, Oliver, help is on the
way," cried Steady Eddie, as he saw
Pandora the Police Car speeding up
the track towards them.

"Right!" called Pandora. "Don't move, you're under arrest."
"What me?" said Oliver Overdrive, quaking on his tyres.
"No, not you, Oliver," said Steady Eddie. "You're not a thief. But you were a fool to be taken in by that red van."

"Anyone could have made that mistake," muttered Oliver Overdrive, as Pandora arrested the van. "Even you, Steady Eddie."

With just a little less of his usual showing off, Oliver Overdrive made his way back to the warehouse with the stolen computers and Steady Eddie drove home.

"Where did you say those computers were taken?" asked Mr Overall, the Depot Manager, who wanted to know every detail of Steady Eddie's exciting day. "Oh, here we go again!" sighed Steady Eddie. "Albatross Avenue, was it? Or Chaffinch Circus? It's on the tip of my tongue . . ."

STEADY EDDIE

I have learned all about road safety. It is very important that you learn all these tips too.

1   Always stop, look and listen before crossing the road. This means stop at the kerb, look for vehicles and listen for sounds of traffic that you may not be able to see coming. When it is safe, you can step off the kerb and cross the road.

2   Try to cross a road with a grown-up you know. Hold their hand while crossing.

3   **Never** run straight across a zebra crossing. Sometimes vehicles are going too fast to stop. Always step carefully on to the crossing when you are sure there is no traffic coming.

4   You must always **walk**, never run, across a road. If you **run** you are more likely to **fall**.

5   Always find a **safe place** to **play**, away from the road.

6   Never cross the road on a corner, the brow of a hill or, if you can help it, between **parked cars**. This is because the driver may not be able to see you and you may not see them.

7   Always **wait** at a pedestrian crossing until the **green person** lights up and you have checked that the **road is clear**. Never cross when the red person is lit up even if you can't see any vehicles approaching.

8   Always wear bright clothing to help the drivers see you, especially in winter when it is dark.

9   Never cross a busy main road unless you can cross safely by using a **pedestrian crossing**, a **zebra crossing**, a **footbridge**, a **subway** or at the **traffic lights**. Make sure that you **know where these safe places are** in the area you live.

10   **Keep safe at all times.** Always tell someone where you are going. Never talk to anyone you **don't know**.

Join the
LITTLE TIGER CLUB
now for lots more
books to enjoy!

Schools can
join too and will
receive a special
enrolment pack.

Join the LITTLE TIGER CLUB now and receive a special Little Tiger goody bag containing
badges, pencils and more! Once you become a member you will be sent details of
special offers, competitions and news of new books. Why not write a book review?
The best reviews will be published on book covers or in the Little Tiger Press catalogue.

The LITTLE TIGER CLUB is free to join. Members can cancel their membership at any
time, and are under no obligation to purchase any books. If you would like details
of the Little Tiger Club, please contact: Little Tiger Press, 22 Manchester Street,
London W1M 5PG, UK. Telephone: 0171 486 0925, Fax: 0171 486 0926
Visit our website at: www.littletiger.okukbooks.com